Linda,

Thank you for meeting with me.

Keep the imagination + education alive!

Preface

When I was eleven years old my aunt suggested I read a book. I told her that I had to read books for school and that books were boring and that I didn't like to read. She was so persistent that I would like the book that I gave in and promised to read it, knowing that I would hate every moment of it. I thought the book had a weird title. *The Hobbit.*

I read the book and fell in love with it. I read everything by J. R. R. Tolkien that I could get my hands on. Then it was time to start creating my own stories. I found that I liked playing the stories out with friends in role playing scenarios more than I actually liked writing. I created two main characters, the second of the two I named "Koldar." I may talk about my first character in a different book. I came up with my first character when I was eleven or twelve, so that would make it about 1980 or 1981. In Koldar's case I had watched a CBS television series called Wizards and Warriors (1983) and in my favorite episode there was a character named Colter. I liked that character and his name so I used that name as inspiration and came up with "Koldar."

I continued (and still continue) to develop my world over the next few years. I named my world Aralon because I had read somewhere that "aralon" meant "peace." By 2000 I had created a very basic website for my world. Real life got in the way and the website remains unfinished to this day, but the basics of my world are there. I even found a background picture I was able to use that had a planet with rings around it in a binary star system just like I had envisioned. Thank you digitalblasphemy.com. The only problem with the picture was that the world was red instead of blue and green, but that was minor compared to the rings and the twin suns.

When I was blessed with children we all played on this world. One of my sons even created a blog about it. Now that my children are older I figured it was time to share my fantasy world with everyone else so I decided to publish a short story based on the origins of my character Koldar.

The story depicts the major events that shaped Koldar's character and his struggle to find purpose in living after significant loss.

Prologue

As he ran through the trees, the twelve-year-old boy hoped beyond hope. "Please Cyros," he prayed quietly, "Let my parents be alive!"

He rushed toward the smoke and flame that he knew was his city. He heard raucous laughter and shouts of victory. He was obliged to hide as a pack of Northmen went by carrying large chests and singing in triumph.

Waiting was almost too much for Koldar, but he dared not be seen by these massive axe-wielding, blond-haired men. As soon as he thought they were far enough away, Koldar dashed toward his home.

It had been destroyed by fire and axe. He frantically looked for signs of life, but there was no trace of his parents. His mother's study was destroyed, her books of magic torn or burnt, there was no gold or silver or . . . gems! *Father!* he thought. *The jewelry store!* He rushed through the ruined streets, not giving heed to the wails and cries of those who were still alive. *Please, Cyros, let my father be alive, and please, dear Surisis, let my mother be with him!* he prayed over and over as he ran.

He thought of the times his mother would teach him the ways of magic, or the times he would go on trips with his father, who taught him the art of swordplay on their way to sell or buy some special gem. He could hardly wait until he was old enough for his father to teach him how to fashion gems into beautiful works of art for use as jewelry or décor, or even for the use of magic. His mother and father worked well together in their respective talents, and they loved each other and him, their only son, Koldar.

Koldar abruptly came to a halt outside his father's jewelry shop, suddenly afraid to enter. It too was destroyed, probably one of the first places hit. But he had to know . . . he rushed in, stumbling over the bodies of some Northmen, and hurried into the back of the store. He saw them as torn apart as the buildings around him—the bodies of his parents. The world spun, the enormity of the loss was overwhelming. His world was literally destroyed.

Pounding in chest, can't breathe, *can't be real* . . . dizziness, throbbing in the head . . . more Northmen voices . . . Were they real, or just nightmarish echoes, sounds of those who had butchered his parents? Where was the light? *Kalaar take me,* he thought as his emotions overwhelmed him, and he blacked out and fell to the floor.

CHAPTER 1

"The outsider," the people in the village called him, and it suited him fine as he did not necessarily want to be associated with these people . . . except for his wife.

He stood outside, in the shadows of his home, his wavy raven-black hair half covering his face, watching his wife and son, Ahrik. The warm firelight from the hearth danced on his wife's lovely face, mesmerizing him with her beauty while also representing her fiery spirit.

How perfect! he thought. *The only two things worth living for, my wife and son . . .*

"Who are Tohar and Rhak?" Ahrik asked his wife.

"Tohar is the god of the sky and leader of all the hahlier under Vicktroath. Rhak is the god of strength, and he . . ." Krysana began.

Ahrik interrupted. "If the hahlier are the servants of the real powers why do we pray to them instead of the real powers they serve?"

The innocent question put a smile on the outsider's face in spite of himself.

Krysana began to answer. "Because, my son . . ."

At this point, the outsider made his entrance. "Hello, my family!"

"Da!" the four-year-old yelled as he jumped up and ran to his father.

The outsider swooped him up in a big bear hug and swung him around and around, saying, "My favorite sound!"

"Hello, my lover," came the quiet, teasing voice of his wife.

"All right, *almost* my favorite sound," he responded playfully. "Have you been telling Ahrik nethersite stories?" He asked as he and Ahrik fell to the ground laughing and wrestling.

"Oh, I wasn't telling him ghost stories. I was teaching him of the gods." For the time being, the outsider ignored the jab and concentrated on wrestling with his son, who was getting quite good at it. It might be time to take him hunting soon. *He'll be the youngest villager to bring down a wolf on his own!*

Soon Krysana said, "All right, Ahrik, time for bed."

After appropriate grunts of disappointment from both father and son, Ahrik hugged and kissed his parents and went off to snuggle in the warmest furs in all of the village.

Krysana came over to her husband, and they touched foreheads and noses. She rubbed the smooth skin of his face with one hand.

"Why don't you like me telling Ahrik about the gods?" she asked.

"Oh, I don't mind you telling him stories about them. I just don't want him to have false hopes that they'll step in and help him. My parents were both very devout and so was I, for a child, and it didn't help any of us."

"The gods are not here to make our lives easy. It is our job to show the gods—and ourselves—how we will act in any given circumstance."

"Why? So we can die someday and live in bliss with these beings who didn't help us while we were down here? I don't believe it."

"Well, one step at a time . . ."

Seeing the kindness and patience Krysana had for him the outsider softened and quietly asked, "How do you put up with me, my love?"

She wrapped her arms around him and roughly pulled him close. "Well, you definitely have your challenges, but I wouldn't have any other man be a father to my Ahrik."

Squeezing her tight, he kissed her, and they melted into each other.

CHAPTER 2

The next day found the outsider digging furiously into the mountainside as fast as he could, partially to keep warm in the snow, but more so because desire, curiosity, and hope drove him. *It didn't fall from the rings . . . I must find it,* he thought as he worked. Then he sensed that something was wrong and he stopped abruptly. The hair on the back of his neck stood up, and he flipped his head around just in time to see a very large white wolf flying through the air at him. He had just enough time to dodge the animal's initial charge, and the two ended up wrestling. He cast a quick glance at his battle axe, it was too far away. It would be no help now as he and the wolf struggled to best each other, in a fight for survival.

* * *

In the warmth of the firelight in the outsider's abode, Ahrik ran around, going from his mother to their visitor, a large older bearded man named Garrin who wore leathers and fur.

Garrin asked Krysana, "Did Koldar say where he was going?"

"He found something on the mountainside and wanted to investigate," she responded, but then a thought struck her. "Although he should have been back a long time ago," she added.

"He'll be fine, I'm sure. Perhaps he is just preparing for the hunt."

There was a sudden blast of cold air as the door flung open. Startled, they all looked at the door.

Koldar stood in the entry, wearing a large white wolf skin over his older furs with a battle axe in one hand and a large bag in the other. He had been wounded, but looked impressive standing in the doorway.

Krysana went from fear to worry as she jumped from her seat and ran to Koldar to inspect his injuries and ask if he was all right. At the same time, Ahrik charged him with an excited cry of "Mi daddy! Mi daddy!"

Reassuring Krysana with a short, hearty laugh and an "I am fine, my love," he dropped his battle axe and bag and picked up Ahrik, who had fastened himself to his leg. He kissed Krysana on her cheek, then stiffened and nodded toward Garrin, who was still sitting in the fur-covered chair watching the scene and trying not to smile. Garrin gravely returned the nod, matching Koldar's mood (more so out of respect for Koldar's feelings than anything else).

Hesitantly and as if forcing out the words, Koldar said, "Hello . . . Father."

Krysana asked what happened, to which Koldar responded, "While I was digging ore for weapons, a snow wolf attacked me. We wrestled, and I ended up killing it with my bare hands."

Garrin got up and studied the wolf skin Koldar was wearing. "Impressive, my son. However, this was a young wolf. The older ones are twice as big."

"What's the matter, *Garrin*? Afraid an outsider might become as good a warrior as a Northman?"

Krysana and Garrin looked at Koldar with disappointment. Koldar's hard emotional shell softened a bit and he said, "I am sorry, Father. It's still hard. I do appreciate everything you have done for me all these years."

"That's understandable, but know that I have loved you as our own from the very beginning."

Koldar nodded in understanding. Garrin reached down to inspect the bag Koldar brought in, saying, "Well now, let's see what we have here."

Koldar quickly closed the bag. "No! It's a . . . a surprise! Come, Ahrik. Let's play!"

Garrin and Krysana exchanged worried looks but seeing that Koldar wouldn't have any more of the discussion they each sat down and watched as Koldar and Ahrik played.

Koldar spent the next day preparing his ore to be smelted. Later that night as Koldar and Krysana were lying in bed together, she quietly called out his name. Koldar absently answered, "Hmm?"

"What's in the bag you brought home? It's just iron ore, isn't it?"

"Oh, it's ore all right, but I have a feeling it's different . . . harder, better."

Krysana's face was thoughtful. Then her eyes opened suddenly with understanding and shock. "Koldar! You didn't go search out that fireball that was sent from the gods, did you?"

"It wasn't a fireball," Koldar answered. "There is some kind of metallic ore in it, and it didn't fall from the rings which surround Aralon. It came from a different direction. There is something about it . . ."

"You shouldn't mess with such things. It was a sacred sign that the hunt should begin!"

"Oh, I don't know if it is all that sacred. It's just a rock that fell from the sky. I doubt very much that the gods sent that for a sign to begin the hunt—we were already preparing for the hunt."

Krysana gasped at the heresy.

"Besides if it did come from the gods, how do you know they didn't put that ore in there on purpose for us to find and thereby become stronger?" Koldar suggested.

"Or to test us to see if we will refrain from using it," Krysana shot back.

"I have been looking for something that will impress the village elders, and I think this may be it," Koldar said as if it was sufficient to end all doubt for Krysana.

"Be careful, Koldar," Krysana said, still unconvinced it was a good idea.

CHAPTER 3

The hammer fell repeatedly upon the anvil. Sparks from the sword filled the smithy. Koldar worked furiously and with a passion as if he were Karr himself forging the bodies of the dwarves. The effort of his work showed in the glistening sweat that covered his shirtless body.

The door behind Koldar opened, letting in a snowy wind. Koldar continued to work, uncaring about the intrusion. Then Garrin's deep voice was heard.

"Ha! Ha! Koldar, my son! You work with the might of a dragon and the speed of a puma and the endurance of a snow wolf. The other smiths have gone home hours ago!"

Koldar, not turning, answered with, "I am almost done."

"I have brought two of the elders with me. They are interested to see your work."

Koldar continued to hammer. After a while, the two elders looked at each other in mutual disapproval of Koldar's disregard for them. Then the hammering stopped. The deathly quiet was almost louder than the ringing of the anvil. There was the sound of a splash, and massive amounts of steam filled the forge. After swishing the sword in the water, Koldar let the steam fade, then spoke.

"Show this to the elders and see if it does not exceed their expectations of an outsider!" he declared as he handed his newly made sword to Garrin.

In the past, Garrin had been exasperated by the fact that Koldar referred to himself as an outsider, but this time, he simply sighed and responded quietly with, "You are not an outsider, my son. We have considered you ours from the time we found you. It is you who must consider yourself a true Northman."

Koldar ignored the comment and gestured for Garrin to show the sword to the elders. It resembled a long sword of the Southerners, not the short, wide blades used by the Northmen. Most Northmen didn't use swords at all. Most use hand, or battle, or great axes.

The elders appeared to be older than Garrin and were wearing leather and furs. One of them took the sword from Garrin and held it up. The three of them inspected it closely. The other elder spoke, saying, "It is finely shaped."

The first one responded with, "Excellent craftsmanship!" He motioned for the others to stand back. He began swinging the blade to and fro. Then he balanced the blade on his finger and announced, "It is very well balanced . . . for a sword."

They all turned and looked at Koldar as the elder handed it back to him and said, "It is a fine piece of work. Possibly stronger than any other Northman blade. You are indeed an asset to our tribe."

Koldar took the sword and nodded respectfully at the elder. Then he handed the sword to Garrin, saying, "I want you to have it, Father, as a symbol of our friendship and growing love."

Well there, I said the word "love" I hope he is happy and I hope that someday I can truly come to love him for all that he has done for me.

Garrin ceremoniously took the sword and said, "Thank you, my son. I will wield it with bravery and honor. Come! Let us show Krysana!"

Koldar got his furs from a hook on the wall, discreetly dropped some on his bag of ore to hide it, clasped his wolf skin about his shoulders and grabbed his battle axe. The four of them exited the smithy.

Steam rose from Koldar's body in great wafts in the cold night air, and Garrin had the thought that the fire of the forge still burned within him.

Garrin and Koldar headed for Koldar's house while the elders went off in a different direction. The two men heard a sound off in the distance, and stopped and strained to listen. It was the steady beat of wind as if large wings were methodically flapping . . . the sound got louder. As it grew closer, they also heard what sounded like splashes and steam. Garrin's eyes suddenly widened with understanding and horror, and he yelled, "Run, Koldar! Run!"

They started running. Dropping the extra furs he was holding, Koldar quickly outdistanced Garrin. The sound was right on top of them now, and shouts and screams of fear from the villagers could be heard. Koldar looked up, and his fear doubled, he dropped and rolled behind a hut. Liquid came from above and burned out part of the wall he was behind. The destructive force passed by Koldar and he started running toward home again. As he ran, scenes of his past life came flashing, unbidden, into his mind. Just as it was so long ago, people were running everywhere. Scorched bodies lay about, some with loved ones crying over them. Koldar's run became desperate.

CHAPTER 4

The strongest Northman in the village slept on the ground in a thick tropical jungle. He suddenly awoke as if from a nightmare. He instinctively looked north and urgently whispered, "Father!" He picked up a very large battle axe, the largest ever known to be made and that could only be wielded expertly by Xar, Garrin's firstborn son, and he started running north.

* * *

As Koldar ran, he spied short, dark thieves taking advantage of the chaos, grabbing what they could and running, being sure to keep clear of the destructive fury.

"Goblins!" Koldar spat as if the word itself were profanity.

Two of the bigger goblins blocked Koldar's way. He deftly hefted his axe, and without too much trouble, he dispatched both of them. Stumbling now in a hurry, he rushed to his home and burst inside. The roof had many holes in it, and several of the walls were partially destroyed. Searching the small house, he saw what looked like two bodies scorched beyond recognition. Close by, he spied a pile of scorched debris, his eyes focused on something that made his heart stop, the burnt remains of one of Ahrik's favorite toys. . . as if Ahrik had been holding it when he died.

"No!" Koldar yelled in horror. He forced himself to walk out of his house, his head in a whirl.

Garrin was close to Koldar's house, fighting several goblins using Koldar's sword. The sword was effective, even though it hadn't yet been fully sharpened. The bodies at Garrin's feet indicated he had been successful thus far in the brawl, but soon the numbers became overwhelming. He yelled out, "Koldar! Koldaar!"

Suddenly, the goblins broke off their attack on Garrin as if even hearing Koldar's name was enough to make them run. Satisfied, Garrin relaxed for just a second and then noticed that the goblins were running toward Koldar's home and looking up behind themselves. Garrin turned to see what they were looking at, cried out in pain, and dropped to the ground, his body half gone, vaporized by powerful, magical liquid acid, the breath weapon of a dragon, a huge dragon black as midnight and powerful as a dozen hurricanes. Koldar watched in horror as the dragon flew on not caring who was killed, not caring that Koldar's adopted father and wife and son had just died.

Yelling in anguish, Koldar dodged another breath attack just in time, but several goblins were not so lucky. Then the dragon swooped back around and landed, grabbing a mouthful of goblins. Koldar, seeing his opportunity, charged the dragon and hit it hard with his battle axe. The blade shattered on the impossibly hard scales of the beast. Uncaring, the beast continued to devour the goblins.

Astonished, Koldar staggered back and grabbed the sword he had just given Garrin. He then leaped onto the tail end of the dragon and ran up its back and plunged the sword deep into the creature's back. The surprised dragon roared in pain and stole a quick look at who had caused the pain. Koldar's and the beast's eyes met just for a moment and each of them knew they had an enemy for life. Koldar pulled the sword from the dragon intending to strike again, but the dragon suddenly reared back, knocking Koldar and his sword to the ground.

Koldar got back to his feet and spat at the dragon in defiance as it took off and flew into the distance. The goblins had disappeared by this point as well.

Koldar, having just lost everything . . . again, could see no point caring about anything anymore, no point in living, no point in moving on. Memories of his wedding flashed through his mind, mixed with the burnt wreckage of his abode. He let himself fall back into the snow, his mind a whirl of images as he welcomed the blackness of sleep.

Koldar awoke sometime later. Opening his eyes, he could see the stars against the night sky with dark clouds moving in, and there was a pain in his chest and gut. A familiar pain, not from any physical wound, but the familiar pain of loss. It was much more acute and robust than it was those many years ago, however, because this time it was his wife and son that he lost.

He tried to move, but the pain had sapped the strength from his whole body. The shock of loss was too great. Images and delirium came at him from every direction as if by a never-ending volley of arrows. He tried to get up, but could not. The pain, the heaviness . . .

Struggling to free himself from the bonds that held him, he roared in agony and only succeeded in curling up in a ball and sobbing uncontrollably. Minutes turned into hours. *Shut it out, shut it out . . .* The only conscious thought he could muster. Finally, exhausted, he let the darkness overtake him again, ignorant of the soft flakes that now began to fall from the sky and land on his exposed skin.

CHAPTER 5

Koldar sat at a tavern in a Southern village. It was cold outside, but there was no snow on the ground. He was wearing leather clothes and had on his wolf fur and had added Garrin's medallion as a fastener to the cloak. It was a metal buckle of sorts, about three inches in diameter, with short axe blades coming off a one-inch circle and all with the interwoven knots of the Northmen. It had been several days since he had shaved.

"A dragon!" exclaimed a tavern patron sitting next to Koldar. "There hasn't been a dragon story told in years. Ha! Ha! Ha! Did he swoop down from nowhere and steal all yer gold? Ha! Ha! Ha!"

Slamming his mug down, Koldar responded, "No, you idiot. He wiped out my entire village."

"Not your entire village! You are still here. Ha! Ha! Ha!"

Then another patron piped up. "I don't think I've ever heard such a tale! I ain't met a barbarian yet that don't have blond hair. You ain't no Northman! Unless'n you're a motherless . . ."

Before the patron could finish his slur Koldar had jumped to his feet and brandished his sword. At first, the patrons readied themselves for a fight, but when they saw Koldar's mangled sword, they all just laughed. Koldar looked at his sword, then dropped it and swung his fists wildly in his inebriated state. There was more laughter.

The next thing, he knew he was being thrown through the door. As he lay there in the muddy street, his mangled sword and his pack were thrown out after him. He tried to get up, and was nearly run over by a horse and wagon.

* * *

Back at the ruined Northman village, Xar knelt by a wooden grave marker that said GARRIN. He stood and looked around. The village was in ruins, and snow partially covered many bodies.

* * *

Koldar sat leaning against a tree in a green forested area, drinking out of a flask and muttering to himself. His furs were much more filthy and matted, and his beard, now long, was wild and tangled. He had the feeling some time had passed since the disaster at the village and the incident in the tavern, but he didn't care much and didn't give it any thought at this point, all he could think of was his alcohol.

Then Koldar heard the sounds of a skirmish just a little way off. There was the clash of steel and grunting, but the sounds were distorted. He thought he heard Garrin's voice, although he couldn't make it out. He clumsily got up to investigate. He picked up his mangled sword and slurred, "Garrin? Ish that you?"

He drunkenly walked over to the edge of a short drop-off. Below him were several figures fighting and yelling. He tried hard to focus on what he was seeing.

"Goshblins!" Koldar spat, his pain turning to anger.

He stumbled over to his flask and splashed liquid on his face in an effort to clear the fog in his head. It didn't have its intended effect, but he went back to the ledge and looked at the battle. There were several figures fighting below. Memories reeled through his mind—Garrin fighting the goblins, the goblins looting and pillaging back at the village, and finding his family, scorched.

"No!" Koldar yelled. He jumped down into the fray and immediately knocked down two goblins. He fought viciously, using his fists and mangled sword. He was not very accurate or deadly, but he did pose a threat.

* * *

Koldar slept peacefully. He was in a delicate bedroom suite with two tall, slender figures bending over him. They were pale and beautiful, dressed in rich greens and silvers, and had pointed ears. The male spoke. "He is waking."

Koldar stirred. "Oh, my head!" He grasped at his temples and forced his eyes open.

The female elf asked politely, "How do you feel?"

Koldar looked at them uncomprehendingly and tried to get up.

"Shhh, Shh don't get up yet." She said reassuringly and Koldar let and his head fall back onto the pillow.

"Like someone is hitting my head with a hammer," Koldar finally responded.

"Here, drink this. It will help."

Koldar hesitated, then took the glass he was offered. He sipped it at first and found that it was quite pleasant. It seemed to fill a void inside him, so he heartily drank the rest of it down.

"I am Lendril," the she-elf offered.

"And I am Galendae," her companion said.

"Ahldain elves," Koldar said matter-of-factly "Of the third family, I would guess."

"That is correct," Lendril responded.

"My mother taught me history and social anthropology. I have just never met one before," Koldar explained.

"You saved my life in the skirmish," Galendae said. "I am in your debt."

"Oh that's nice," Koldar said absently, still trying to gain some kind of focus, "Now can you tell me something? Where am I?"

"Well, after that little encounter in the woods," Galendae answered, "I found you passed out. So I brought you to our haven. My sister is a skilled physician, and she has taken care of you the past few days."

"You have been asleep ever since you came," Lendril interjected. "My enchantments put you in a healing sleep. How do you feel now?"

"I am starting to feel pretty good, actually. What is the date?"

Galendae answered the query. "By the human calendar, it is the eighteenth day of the fourth month in the year 386 I. D."

"386 I.D! Are you sure?" Koldar asked in surprise.

"Yes, quite positive."

"Well then, I guess I feel great for not knowing where a whole year of my life went!" Koldar looked at Lendril and felt a flash of pain at a memory of his wife's face. Shaking his head of the vision he asked, "Have I been here for a whole year!?"

"No," Lendril answered smiling, "As we said, you have only been here a few days, ever since the skirmish. Where you were before that I have no idea."

"Why don't you rest now?" Lendril suggested.

Koldar's head began to swim with memories. Pain ripped out his heart, and he began having a hard time breathing. "Do you have any ale?" Koldar asked desperately.

Lendril shook her head.

"How about wine, then? I bet elves have great wine!"

"Alcohol is not the proper way to deal with your trials," Lendril said. "Why don't you start by telling me what's bothering you?"

At this point, Galendae quietly left the room.

"I don't want to!" Koldar spat out. He was still having a hard time breathing, and now started to get angry as well. Lendril started chanting calmly. She took a leaf and dipped it into a nearby bowl that had a light-gray muddy substance in it. She then smeared the substance on Koldar's forehead, and he began to calm down a little.

"Now, tell me what is wrong."

Being overcome with emotion and not finding an outlet in alcohol Koldar started to sob and slowly began to speak. "When I was young a group of barbarians attacked our town and killed my family. A second tribe of Northmen found me and took pity on me . . ."

Koldar continued to tell his tale, moving through the emotions until he ended with, ". . . and then I woke up here."

Lendril gently helped Koldar lie back down. Emotionally exhausted, Koldar closed his eyes and fell asleep.

CHAPTER 6

Koldar walked down the corridor with determination. He wore elven garb, and his beard had been nicely trimmed. He had remained clean-shaven while in the Northman village as an additional sign that he was an outsider, but now he decided to wear a beard to honor them, but he kept it trimmed. Galendae joined him from an adjoining hall.

"Ah, Koldar. You seem to be feeling better."

"I am, thank you."

"Is there anything I can do for you?"

"Actually, there is.

Before he could continue they were interrupted by the sound of a horn blowing.

"The Haven is under attack!" Galendae shouted.

They ran as Galendae drew his sword. Others bustled about them, preparing and rushing to defend The Haven.

Koldar and Galendae burst out into the courtyard. The goblins had broken into the elven haven and were accompanied by larger fell beasts. The elves were barely holding them at bay due to the sheer number of assailants. Galendae rushed to join his companions while Koldar watched briefly. Memories rushed back to him of the goblins during the attack on the Northman village, it seemed like it was just yesterday. Rage welled up within him, but he kept control of himself and used the anger to focus. He rushed into the fray and knocked out a goblin with his fist, then picked up an elven blade from a dead elf. The blade glowed a pale shimmering green, and he began the work of death among the beasts.

* * *

Several hours later the goblins had been routed and Koldar found himself in the throne room of The Haven. The room was made of natural foliage expertly interwoven with stonework. The stone offered protection while not intruding on the beauty of nature. Elves dressed in their best attire were performing some kind of ceremony before the throne. They came to a stop, and then the elven king commanded, "Koldar, come forward!"

The circle of elves parted, revealing Koldar to the king. Koldar was dressed in elven ceremonial garb with his cleaned white wolf skin draped over his shoulders, proudly displaying his adopted father's clasp. The elven elegance of his garb seemed a direct contrast with the wild ferocity of the wolf skin, but Koldar wore it well. Koldar walked forward solemnly and knelt before the king.

The elven king rose from his throne, approached the kneeling man, and spoke. "Koldar, no human in these past four hundred years has shown bravery or honor to our tribe as thou hast. This ceremony, held in your honor, will be complete upon your answering the following question: Do you promise to up-hold this kind of bravery and honor to all elves in good standing?"

Koldar soberly answered with a "Yes," to which the elven king said,

"Lower thine head."

When Koldar did so, the king drew his sword and touched Koldar with it three times. Then two elves walked forward, took the sword from the king, and handed him a silver circlet with an emerald set at its front center. The king placed the circlet on Koldar's head and said, "Then I hereby name thee 'elf friend,' the highest honor we can bestow upon any man."

The king then spoke in his native tongue, and the circlet dissolved into Koldar's head. A few moments passed, then the circlet emerged from Koldar's head, now ethereal in nature. It seemed to shimmer and was actually not touching his head, but hovered an inch or two above his skin.

"This circlet," the king continued, "can only be seen by elves in good standing with Ahslyanus, the father of the elves. If you should ever knowingly harm an elf, the circlet will turn black and show you for the betrayer you are."

"Thank you, Your Majesty," Koldar responded as he had been previously instructed to say.

"Now, how may we repay you for such bravery in defending our haven?" asked the king.

Koldar paused, then raised his head and said, "Oh, mighty king. I ask for time and knowledge. The knowledge I seek is known to no man, and I swear by my honor as elf friend never to divulge it if it should be made known to me."

"And what may that be?"

"Your Majesty, if it pleases you, I desire to know the secrets of the process of elven blade making, for which knowledge I will give unto thee a metal harder, stronger, and sharper than steel."

"My naïve friend," said the king, "were we to show you this, you could not master it, as it takes a skill greater than you possess."

"Yes, my lord. This is why I also asked for time. Time to retrieve something and to study at your swordsmiths' hands."

"And what is this thing you must go retrieve?" asked the king. "The Gift of Surisis!" Koldar answered boldly, and all the elves gasped in astonishment.

CHAPTER 7

Koldar stood outside the ruins of his nativity. The stone wall around the city was mostly intact, but the gate was smashed, and he could see the damaged structures within the walls from where he stood. He was dressed in the garb from his Northman village. He wore a chain mail shirt with a black leather pauldron on his left shoulder. He also wore his wolf skin and some elven accessories, including an elven long blade at his side.

From the looks of it, no one had attempted to rebuild the city. They probably all felt it was too close to the Northman lands. It was one of the few cities of its kind. Cities, especially human cities, were rarer after the invasion of the dwarves almost four hundred years ago. Humans mostly live in scattered villages now. The fact that this city was built so shortly after the dwarven armistice showed great determination and ingenuity, and that it lasted so long was a tribute to the philosophies espoused by the people there. Most of them worshiped Cyros, the god of light and truth, he is considered to be the son of Ahl. He was also credited for placing the twin suns in their positions.

The thought of his childhood and of Cyros almost made Koldar smile, but then the wind changed slightly and the stench of decay, rot, and death from the city filled his nostrils. He spat on the ground. "Cyros! Ha!" He looked up and shouted at the sky, "Where were you when your people were slaughtered by the sons of Tohar? Light and truth didn't stop a passion for victory and the greed of Sortfynas . . . Your angels are wasted on me Cyros!"

Then Koldar had a thought. *I bet the people of the tribe that slaughtered my parents say they worship Tohar or Rhak or even Viktroath, but they do the work of Sortfynas and Dradok. I bet Sortfynas and Dradok both grow stronger in the deeds of that clan. Too bad Viktroath doesn't care to stop the raids . . . Ah! Gods? What am I saying? They don't care!*

The city gate attached to the stone wall was once impressive and protected against many would-be assailants—goblins, ogres, and other fell beasts and men—but the Northman clan was quick and strong and deadly. They gained the upper hand and pushed forward as if Dradok himself were leading them into battle. Now the city belonged to Kalaar, the god of death. *Humph!* Koldar thought ironically. *It was probably Kalaar's idea to take the city.*

As he started to go through the destroyed city gates, a rush of memories and emotions hit him hard. He focused on making anger replace the sorrow, the empty void that had been his constant companion since his parents' death. In fact, he would call on Pyron now to help fan the flames of his fury if he thought that Pyron would listen to him, but he knew that Pyron, the god of hate, didn't care. He had to do this on his own. He filled the void with his rage and knew that the only way he could get revenge and to stop that dragon from hurting other people was to get The Gift of Surisis.

Using his rage as a guide and a ward against "what could have been," he walked through the streets, ignoring the rubble, scurrying rodents, decay and bones that were there and focused only on finding The Gift. He finally reached his neighborhood and had to stop and think. Where would The Gift be? Was his mother wearing it when they attacked? He decided that could not be the case because if so, the greedy barbarians wouldn't have stood a chance. Was it possible that a thief had taken it? Yes, that was a possibility, but not if his mother had placed it in her secret hiding spot. Suddenly he knew which way to turn. He headed for his house. Darkness and despair threatened to overpower him as he neared it, but he kept a silent anger and stayed focused.

Yeah, Kalaar I bet you would love for me to collapse and die here. Well, I asked you to take me all those years ago, and you didn't. You lost your chance to have me! He reached his home. As he stepped over the threshold, tears and a sob came unbidden, but they were not the tears of total despair and blackness, just the healthy release of pain. He let the tears flow as he looked in his mother's study. Almost everything was gone. Any trickster who thought he could learn magic would have taken her spell books . . . Hmmm.

But the secret to where she hid The Gift was not in a spell book. She would often write her "learnings" in a journal. These learnings were philosophical in nature and therefore did not have anything a would-be spell caster could use. He looked frantically now for the book. It was not in the study, so he moved to the dining room. It was not there either. "By the suns!" he exclaimed. "Where could it be?"

Then he remembered. He had been reading it the night before the barbarian raid. That was what had inspired him to go into the forest the next day to look for plants that could be used as spell components. That book saved his life then, and now he was hoping it could be the means of avenging his wife and son . . . and adopted father.

He rushed into his old room, the tears flowing harder now and the sobs stronger. Black despair knocked at the sides of his consciousness, but he focused on the task at hand, and the future . . . the future justice he hoped to get. His bed had been slashed and the legs broken. It smelled like something had died recently in the sheets. Plugging his nose, he picked up debris until he found it—his mother's learning journal.

Ignoring the stench, he sat down and began to pore over the book. His sobs subsided as he embraced the happy memories he had of reading it alone in his room and together with his loving mother. He read about Aralon's sister planet, which was destroyed during the God Wars. He read of the sacred and powerful Life Crystals owned by each of the gods, and the Life Crystal placed in the center of Aralon and of its older sister planet. He read how the dwarves were created by Karr and brought to life by Ahl to be sturdy and hardy so they could dig in the older planet and find the Life Crystals that had been stolen from the good gods.

He read how the planet was destroyed and the debris of it formed rings around Aralon. He read how sometimes the remains of the planet shone like any other planet in the binary solar system, but sometimes didn't depending on which broken side of the cracked planet faced Aralon as it still spun and rotated around the suns. "The disappearing star," children would call it. He read of the elven star stones and how they were used against humans and elves when the traitorous dwarves invaded this continent. He read how Surisis created a powerful artifact to aid Ahl's children in their effort to stem off evil. *Ah-ha! Here it is*, Koldar thought.

The words were not written in the language of magic, but after the manner of the high elves, the Ahldain elves of the first family. Elven script and words, but a magical incantation. *Oh, Mother, you were brilliant!* Koldar recognized the writing. It was one of the first incantations she had taught him. He rubbed his eyes, clearing out the last of the tears, then closed his eyes in preparation. Opening them he began to read, softly at first, but then louder and louder until the incantation had finished. His eyes were forced shut by the power of the spell, and when he opened them again, everything around him was ghostly in appearance.

He could see where the walls of the home were and the rubble around him, but he could also see through them. Closing the book and putting it under his arm, he stood up and looked around. He saw a light shining in his direction. It looked like it came from their old garden. He made his way toward it, walking around the wraithlike walls and over ghostly debris.

Once he was outside, he noticed that the trees had the same see-through appearance. The light appeared to be coming from under their peach tree, about four feet deep. He marked the spot in his mind, for the spell was fading. He let the spell dissipate, and all around him appeared normal again. He would never have known that something was buried four feet below where he was standing.

He dug and dug until his shovel hit something hard. Digging around it, he discovered a stone box about three feet by two feet by one foot. It was heavy even for Koldar, and he figured that most men would not be able to move it very easily. There were no seams or hinges or breaks. Each side was perfectly smooth—he could find no way to open it.

He went back to his mother's journal and re-read the history of Surisis, the goddess of magic, giving her artifact to mankind. Then a thought struck him. *I don't believe the gods hear our prayers or help us, and here I am looking for an artifact called The Gift of Surisis. Will I be able to use it if I don't have faith in the gods? As I recall, it is an item of magic, not faith. Perhaps it is her way of helping us so she doesn't have to listen to our prayers. Now, how to open this box?*

He read the history over and over and could find nothing about a box. Then a passage stood out at him. "The key to The Gift is to pray."

Seriously? I am supposed to pray?

Koldar prayed out loud to Surisis and asked her to open the box. Nothing happened. He tried saying the prayer differently, different words, louder, softer . . . nothing. "I knew it. The gods don't hear us."

Out of frustration and despair, he put his hand on the box, hung his head, and found himself muttering in the language of the magi, "Surisis, open this box." To his astonishment, his hand began to glow blue. Then the light extended to the whole box, a seam appeared around the upper portion, and then the light disappeared, but the seam remained.

"Ah!" Koldar said. "It was an incantation after all, not a prayer. Prayers are never offered in the language of magic—that was just a clue about how to say the incantation!" He picked up the lid and set it aside. In the box was another box seemingly made of pure gold. *Ah, I wonder if this is kahldrite. Kahldrite is supposed to be stronger than steel, but has the appearance of gold. It is very rare, and is supposedly a gift given only to the dwarves by Karr. I doubt very much that a dwarf made this box. I wonder if kahldrite is stronger than my ore.*

Koldar unfastened the lid and opened the golden box. There were two items in it. The Gift of Surisis was there, along with the weather medallion his father used to wear. Koldar smiled. His father would use the medallion to adjust the weather on their trips to ensure a favorable journey. The story of how his father got the medallion made him laugh out loud, but he had no time to reminisce.

He held up The Gift and looked at it. It was beautifully elegant, hanging on a thin chain of elven silver. It was a clear gem about two inches in length in the shape of a teardrop that sparkled in the light. The edges of the gem were covered in a slim border of elven silver. He could feel the power of the artifact as he held it in his hands. He removed his wolf skin and proceeded to take everything off his upper body so he was bare from the waist up. He took The Gift and carefully put it on while muttering the second set of words which were in his mother's book.

The gem was warm and pulsated with energy on his chest. He felt power course through his entire body. Then the gem and the chain began to meld into his skin until they disappeared from sight. He looked down, pleased that it worked. *I'm pretty sure even the Ahldain elves won't be able to see this.* Then he also put on his father's weather pendant, hanging from a black leather strap. It was crafted of bronze and roughly oblong in shape, and it had the weather rune engraved on it. *Barbarian magic!* Koldar mused with a grin. *More crude than elven magic, but still effective.*

Then Koldar, re-dressed and feeling energized, began his trek back to the elven haven.

CHAPTER 8

Sparks flew once again as the familiar sound of Koldar at work filled the elven smithy. Over the past several months, he had been working with the elves. He had enough ore with him to make a dagger, which was perfect to see if he could learn the elven art of making blades. Finally Koldar finished his work and held up the dagger he'd been working on. It was slightly curved after the manner of elves, but it had a saw-tooth feature at the base of the cutting edge and a finger notch below the teeth. The grip was covered with dyed green leather. The bolster and the pommel were roughly hammered silver.

Galendae said, "You know, we could smooth out that silver on the bolster and the pommel."

"No, I made it that way on purpose. I know elegance and grace are elven traits, but that is not me," Koldar said with a smirk. "Let's see how the magic works with my special ore."

Galendae proceeded to blindfold Koldar. Opposite Koldar was a spinning wheel with a filthy piece of black rag on it. The other two elven smiths who assisted Koldar stood expectantly. The first elf said, "Well, Galendae, let's see how good your student is!"

The other elf responded with, "Or perhaps we shall see how good a teacher Galendae is instead!" to which they both laughed.

"Very funny Alanthulus," Galendae shot back.

Galendae then approached Koldar, "Now remember the magic, Koldar. If you truly possess the knowledge, the dagger you made will fly true and strike the goblin cloth. Are you ready?"

Koldar nodded.

The three elves quieted down and watched. Koldar raised his dagger in preparation to throw it. It began to glow a pale green. Galendae's eyes widened with anticipation. Then Koldar threw the dagger at the spinning wheel, making a loud thud. He quickly took off his blindfold to see that the dagger had struck the dead center of the cloth. After a moment of quiet shock, the elves broke into laughter and congratulated him, then proposed they go celebrate with some wine.

"You go ahead." Koldar laughed. As everyone else left, he turned and looked at the dagger, and in deep thought, he took it off the wheel.

* * *

Koldar made his way into the ruined Northman village. The snow was starting to melt with spring right around the corner. He made his way to where he had stabbed the dragon. He allowed himself to recall the night, but only guardedly. He did not let the memories control him. He used them to renew his resolve to destroy the dragon. Then he noticed something sticking out of the snow— something shiny. He bent down, picked it up, and studied it. It was black and slightly bigger than Koldar's outstretched hand.

"Shed a few scales, did we, Blackey?" Koldar said as he picked up another and another of varying size. *It's too bad the new scales are fully formed before the old ones fall off keeping your scale armor impenetrable . . . until now.* Koldar allowed himself a brief smirk.

Eventually, he made his way to the forge. With his arms full of scales, he kicked the door open, walked in, and took a look around. He saw the fur right where he had left it. Lifting the fur, he uncovered his bag of ore.

He took one of the round wooden shields off the wall and lit the forge. He began to experiment with putting the dragon scales on the face of the shield.

Busy and focused on his work, he did not notice the soft sounds of footpads in the snow. Suddenly, the door flew open, and a large snow wolf rushed in and struck at Koldar as another came in behind it. Cursing to himself that he had not latched the doors Koldar fended them off with the heated prongs, but the wolves were smart in maneuvering about the forge, and Koldar could see this wasn't going well.

Then he heard a shout, and one of the wolves fell dead. A large Northman stood in the doorway with the biggest axe ever known to be wielded by man. He wore a fur loincloth, fur boots with leather straps, a large fur cape on his back, and that was it. His massive muscles were bursting at the thrill of a good fight.

"Xar!" Koldar yelled enthusiastically.

The two of them make quick work of the other wolf, then they finally had time to greet each other. Grabbing each other by their right forearms they yanked each other close and patted each other on the back.

Pulling away slightly, Xar said, "I thought you had died with the rest of the village! What happened here, little brother?"

Xar was Garrin's only son. Garrin's wife had died by the time they found the twelve-year-old Koldar in the ruins of his city. Koldar had always liked Xar, who was a couple of years older, and the two of them got along well. Xar was big, even for a Northman, and Koldar often thought that he could rearrange the Constral Mountains if he wanted to. They called themselves brothers, and if anyone ever said they didn't look anything alike, Xar would open his eyes wide. Pointing between his eyes and Koldar's, he would say, "Look! We both have blue eyes. Of course we are brothers!"

"A dragon, black as night, attacked the village," Koldar responded. "My guess is that it was searching for the tribal treasury."

"That's what I thought when I found the dragon scales that had been shed, but I could scarcely believe it. Why did the dragon leave without taking the treasure?" Xar asked.

"I stung him with a special sword. The dragon's acidic blood mangled the sword, but my guess is he had never had any blade pierce his hide before. How do you know he didn't get the treasure?"

"Come, Koldar," Xar said gravely. "I have discovered something this past year and a half."

Koldar and Xar hiked into the forest and up a hill carrying torches. They came to a stone outcropping, and Xar brushed the snow from it. He reached into a fur pouch and took out a silver key.

"I found this while searching through the rubble," Xar explained.

He felt around then found what he was looking for. Keeping his right hand on the rock to mark the keyhole, which was invisible to sight, he inserted the key and turned it. There was a loud clang, and Xar let go. The key began to be pulled into the stone. There was a burst of air that came from behind the rock, revealing its roughly round shape. Then he motioned to Koldar. "Help me move this stone!"

The stone was large and heavy, and normally required three large Northmen to move it. Xar had tried to move it on his own, but he just wasn't able to. But now with Koldar's help, he was hopeful. They strained at the rock, putting all of their might into it. At first Koldar thought they weren't going to succeed, but then . . . movement! That slight success put a shot of adrenaline through them, and they pushed even harder. Eventually, they succeeded in moving the stone from the entranceway. Xar smiled to himself, proud of his strength, then whispered, "For you, Father!" Turning to Koldar, he said, "Come. Let's see what the dragon was after."

They walked through the stone opening, crouching and going single file. Koldar wondered if Xar's massive muscles would prevent him from going through the passageway, but they went on and on. Finally, the tunnel opened up into a natural cavern. Xar stopped abruptly, and Koldar almost ran into him.

"Wait!" Xar commanded. Koldar peered around Xar's massive form and saw a large pile of gold, jewels, gems, and silver on the other side of the cavern.

"You know my father was a rich gem merchant," Koldar said, amazed. "I bet half of this is his."

"Maybe," Xar responded, "but this is the result of years of raids."

"Brother, we can build an army with this!" Koldar began to feel excitement build within him.

"And do what with it?"

"Track down and destroy that dragon!" Koldar said as if it was the most obvious thing in the world, but with determination and vision that ignited Xar's imagination. "Let's go get it!"

"Wait!" Xar commanded again. "Something isn't right." He looked around the cavern. Then he saw it. "Look, Koldar. Do you see that engraving up there on the ceiling?"

Koldar looked up and saw a pattern consistent with the Northmen symbology, an interwoven design of serpents or dragons, sometimes called a knot. It covered the whole roof of the cavern. "Yeah, I see it. Xar, what am I looking at?"

"Well, it's hard to see, as it is very carefully woven into the design, but if you look at the center of it, you can see the rune of hiding."

Looking closer now, Koldar was finally able to pick out the rune. "Ah! Yes, I see it there."

Koldar picked up a rock and tossed it partway out in front of them. It disappeared into the ground, and after a brief moment, they heard it land with a soft thud.

"Ah! An illusion! Very clever," Koldar said. "Wait here and guard the treasure. I will be right back."

"Where are you going?" Xar demanded.

"I'll just be a few minutes!" he shot back as he hurried as best as he could through the passageway.

A few minutes later, Koldar returned. He handed Xar a small silver disk about three inches in diameter. It was so polished that Xar could see himself in its reflection. "I found this in the ruined home of one of the matrons," he explained. "Can you break it?"

"Well, yeah, but . . ."

"All right, break it when I nod at you," Koldar interrupted.

"But . . ." Xar started to protest, however Koldar had closed his eyes and began to speak in a funny language. Then he opened his eyes, and continued to speak. He looked at Xar and nodded. Xar put the disk on the ground and then smashed the butt of his axe onto it with such force that Koldar felt the ground tremble. The disk cracked into three uneven pieces, and Koldar stopped chanting.

They both looked as the ground in front of them began to dissolve, revealing a large pit about twenty feet deep. The pit had several eight-foot spears jutting up from the bottom so that anyone falling would be impaled. Koldar did notice bones at the bottom of the pit. Some were animal in nature, probably unfortunate enough to sneak in when the stone was away from the opening, but others were definitely human. There was one path that made its way to the treasure. It hugged the right side of the cavern and was just barely wide enough for one person.

"I studied magic with my mother before she died," Koldar explained. "I know a few things."

Xar just stared at Koldar for a moment. Then accepting that Koldar could do some magic he smirked and said, "Alright, what's next?"

"Let's leave the treasure here and come back when we need it," Koldar suggested. "It has been safe this whole time—it will continue to be safe."

"What about the hiding spell you broke?" Xar asked.

"Oh, I didn't break the spell. I only allowed our eyes to see past it. If anyone else were to walk in right now, they would see the same solid ground that you and I saw when we first got here. My discovery spell will wear out, so the next time we come back, we will see the solid floor as before, we'll have to remember where we can walk."

They did decide to take some treasure with them so they both carefully made their way to the pile and grabbed what they could at which point Koldar blurted out,

"Come! Let me introduce you to my elven friends at their haven, they are going to help me with some weapons!"

"Elves! Well, let me escort you there, but I think I will let the elves be. They are too sly, treacherous and frail for my taste!"

"Treacherous!? Have you ever met an elf?"

"No! I would like to keep it that way!"

"Alright my brother – but I recommend you keep an open mind." *It's harder to be prejudice if you actually meet and interact with them . . .*

CHAPTER 9

Koldar and Xar gathered the rest of the ore from the meteor and put it and as many dragon scales as they could find in a wagon they had found and repaired in the village. The ore was heavy but they took turns pulling the wagon as they headed south toward The Haven. Each day they would travel into the night, but Koldar still took time to fashion a pauldron out of some of the dragon scales they had gathered. He got little sleep but his determination to rid the world of that black dragon empowered him. He also fashioned a tunic and designed a simple coat of arms that he hung from his belt and carved onto his pauldron with his new dagger. Since the dragon fueled his passion he thought it fitting to have his coat of arms be an image of the very dragon itself. He called himself "Koldar of the Black Dragon" from then on to remind everyone (including himself) of his mission.

The more south they went the closer together the trees became, at one point they began to hear voices some distance away through the trees. The voices were pleading. They sneaked through the trees to see if they could get a closer look.

On a little-used road, there was a long bedraggled caravan, with many different types of wagons all in some state of disrepair which had been stopped. There were four heavily armed men standing at the head of the caravan, and a dirty, ragged man kneeling on the ground in front of them.

"Please, sir, we are displaced. Our crops were killed this year from the blight, we are hungry, and are just looking for a new place to live. The ground has not been good to us these many years. We have only enough to get all of us by for another day or so, and then . . ." his voice trailed off as he realized he could not voice the outcome of running out of food.

"Ah, you do have some food then! Very good! Hand it over, and we will let you live!" One of the men laughed.

"Hey, I think I recognize that laugh," Koldar whispered to his brother.

The kneeling man continued, "To give you our food would be to kill us, and we have no idea where we are going to find a new place to live."

"It's your choice. Die by the sword now, or out of hunger later."

"I can't stand hurtful disregard for others," Koldar said to Xar. He was thinking of the Northmen who raided the city of his nativity, and the goblins and the dragon. *This man is no different from them.*

Anger welled up in Koldar as the bandit raised his sword. A woman behind him screamed, and a child cried out, "Papa!"

Not having enough time to reach the men, Koldar found a stone, threw it at the bandit, and yelled, "Hey! Don't bother the peasants!" The rock hit the man and bounced off his helmet. It was a simple metal helmet, only covering from the eyebrows up, with a nose guard that hung down.

The bandit lowered his sword and looked to see where the stone had come from.

By this time, Koldar was walking out of the trees. Yes, he recognized the man. He had been in the tavern the night Koldar was thrown out.

Koldar drew his elven longsword and put on his round wooden shield with dragon scales on the front of it. He wore his chain mail shirt over his new tunic with his dragon scaled pauldron on his left shoulder and his old black leather pauldron on his right. He also wore a black leather helmet in the style of the Northman with nose and cheekbone guards. Xar remained hidden. The men looked at Koldar, who unstrapped his helmet and threw it to the ground, exposing his wavy black hair.

"Hey, look, Tog! It's that black-haired Northman from the tavern!" the man said, and the four armored men all laughed.

"Have you come to tell us more stories about your dragon?" one of them shot at him.

"No. I just came to help my friend!" Koldar replied as he nodded in the direction of the man on his knees.

"What? This is your friend? Oh, I am so sorry. If I'd have known that, I would have killed him already." And with that, the bandit punched the man hard in the face with the pommel of his sword, never taking his eyes off Koldar. The woman screamed as the man fell to the ground unconscious.

"You've done enough!" Koldar shot back. "Go home!"

"I am afraid we can't do that," he responded.

Koldar felt pain in his left shoulder. An arrow had partially penetrated his chain mail shirt. He didn't know where it came from, as none of the men he was looking at had bows, but he knew he had to take out the ringleader. Through the pain, he put up his shield and charged the armored men. Several arrows had bounced off his shield by the time he reached them. The woman dragged her unconscious husband back away from the men who were now all focusing on Koldar.

The ringleader charged at Koldar, and their swords clashed in the rays of the suns that were streaming through the trees. Two others rushed up, and Koldar was obliged to take on all three. With the number of hits his shield was taking, he was glad it had the dragon scales on it. The fourth man wielded a couple of hand axes and he came around to hit Koldar from behind, but the child who had yelled for his father stepped on this fourth bandit's foot, surprising him and making him miss Koldar. The man turned to kill the boy, but the boy was already running, and the last thing that man saw was Xar's massive hulk looming before him right before Xar's axe cut him down.

Seeing two strong warriors defending them gave hope to the other destitute men in the caravan. They grabbed their pitchforks and shovels and hooks and ran into the forest to find the archers who were still taking potshots at Koldar and Xar, but they weren't hitting their mark as they were also trying to not hit their companions, which is what Koldar had hoped would happen.

Koldar and Xar made quick work of the other three men and then ran into the forest to help hunt down the archers. Koldar had hoped to take one alive, but the archers either fled or were killed by the men from the caravan. Some of those men were badly hurt by arrows or sword wounds. Koldar and Xar did what they could to help bind the wounds and apply healing balm.

The man who had been knocked out came to and assisted with the cleanup. Koldar learned that he was called Spit Thurgood.

When everything was taken care of, he stopped to talk to Koldar. "Thank you for risking your life to save us strangers."

"Ah, it's nothing. These lands have become overrun with beasts and foul men such as this. Head southwest toward the ocean. You should find a spot there."

"Thank you, but that is too far we shall perish before we get there." Spit responded.

Spit's boy came running up and gave Koldar a big hug around his legs. He reached down and patted his head.

"You have a sharp lad there," Koldar said. "My brother tells me that he saved my life." He knelt on one knee to be at eye level with the boy. "Thank you, my lad," he said in earnest. Then he reached into a pouch and pulled out a small gem, bright blue, which sparkled in the setting suns' rays. "Here, take this and help your people become strong with it," he said as he handed it to the boy.

The boy took it, then simply said, "You teach us to be strong."

"Oh, no!" Koldar protested. "I have my own problems to deal with."

"What's the matter, Koldar?" Xar asked. "You said you wanted an army."

"Yes, but not . . ."

"Who are you going to get in these badlands—the group called the Forsaken? Or that pitiful band of men led by Andrek who think they are knights? Or perhaps these elf friends of yours? Come on,

Koldar. The badlands of the Shadow Mountains need someone like you to help tame and civilize them."

"Civilize? Oh no, not me!"

"Come on, brother. These people need you."

Koldar thought about it for a while. He hated those who took advantage of the weak, and this land was full of them, beasts and men alike. If he let these people go now, they would just be set upon by another marauding group. Even in the past year, what civilization was in these lands had been lost.

"All right," he finally said.

The boy let out a "yippee," then stood at attention and saluted Koldar.

"If we are going to bring civilization to these lands, it won't be done by me, but I will do what I can." He then turned to the people and said, "What say you? Do you want to learn to be strong and take care of yourselves? Are you willing to work hard and protect each other?" The people all shouted in approval, and now Koldar had two goals. Kill the dragon, and help the helpless. A surge of excitement went through him in spite of himself.

"All right, but if we do this," Koldar continued, "there will be no jealousies or prejudices! We help all who want it."

"Except for dwarves, obviously," one man commented matter-of-factly.

Koldar turned and looked right at the man, staring at him with a look that made the man shudder. "Even dwarves! We will not judge an individual based on the past actions of an entire nation."

Then he continued louder so everyone could hear. "If a dwarf is destitute or in need of help, we help them. We help everyone, or I walk away right now! What say you?"

They hesitated, so Koldar continued, "We are all on this planet together. No one else will help us."

"What about the gods?" someone called out.

"No one will help you! We help ourselves, and then in turn we help all others in need! What say you?" he yelled.

"We help ourselves, and then we help others!" Spit Thurgood yelled. He turned around to the others of the caravan and said it again and again, starting a chant until the whole caravan was saying it.

Xar whispered to Koldar, "Looks like you have some work to do."

"Aye. What have I gotten myself into?"

After some rest and something to eat the leaders of the caravan sat with Koldar and Xar on the ground in a circle in the woods just a stone's throw from the caravan. The suns had set and they had a small fire going.

Koldar told them of the ruined city where he was born. He told them it would be a lot of work to get it cleaned up and to defend it, but he couldn't think of a better place. He arranged to have Xar lead them there and start the work. His plan was to go back to the elven haven and complete what he had started before joining them at the ruins. He also arranged to have a message sent to his cousin Elkar, who was living in Ahnor closer to the sea.

"He is my father's brother's son, and he is the one who will bring civilization to these lands," Koldar said.

CHAPTER 10

Koldar made his way back to the elven haven with the cart full of ore and scales, leaving the caravan refugees in Xar's capable hands.

Keeping his promise, he gave the elven king most of the special ore and kept enough for himself to make a sword and a spear.

Koldar and Galendae and the other elves worked night and day. Koldar worked with a passion that amazed the elves. They would come into the forge in the morning to find him still there, working away, utilizing magic and metal.

As Koldar's project was nearing completion, Galendae said to him, "This magic still won't protect the blades from the dragon's acid. The ore is strong enough to pierce the scales and the magic will aid in that, but the acid will still hurt the weapons. If you want the weapons protected, you must use the dragon's own essence."

Koldar thought for a moment, then said, "Go to your mystic. Ask her when and where would be the best place to gather this essence. Find out if there is a way it can be gathered without another run-in with the beast."

Several days later, Galendae came running into the forge. "I have news, Koldar, but you must leave now!"

Koldar doused his work in the water and hurried to follow Galendae.

"It took quite a bit of time and talent," Galendae continued as they ran toward The Haven's gate, "but the mystic discovered that the dragon you hunt has made a temporary home in a cavern. The journey will be long, and once you get there, you must wait for her to leave."

"Her?" Koldar asked.

"Yes. She has laid eggs and she will fly off in search of food for her hatchlings. The window of time will be very small, so when she leaves, you will have to hurry."

"This world doesn't need *more* of those beasts," Koldar muttered to himself.

"Hurry, Koldar! The mystic has drawn a map of how you can get to her cavern. It lies northeast of here in the heart of the shadow of the rings, and I have gathered gear and food for you by the gate."

* * *

After traveling for weeks, scrounging what he could off the land to eat, climbing ever higher and higher in the mountains, Koldar felt like he was finally getting close. The stench in this place was horrid. Koldar almost lost what little food he had eaten for lunch it was so bad, but he recognized the smell. Memories of that awful night came flooding back to him, and he utilized the memories to drive him forward. He climbed up and peered over a ledge, and there he saw it—a cavern opening. *That's got to be it. Now I wait.* He went back down a few feet and sat down on a ledge just out of sight of the opening. He hoped the dragon was far enough inside that she wouldn't smell him—otherwise, this was a one-way trip. The wind was blowing the right direction, so he took his chances and settled in to wait.

Dawn broke the morning of the fourth day since he had taken up his position. The fear had long been replaced by boredom. Then all of a sudden, the sky turned black, and wind drove past him so fiercely that he had to steady himself against being blown over the edge. *There she goes,* he thought. *I guess the thrust of her wings pushed all the air my way so she still doesn't smell me. Now's my chance!*

He waited until she was out of sight, and then scrambled up the rock cliff. As he rounded the top, he was almost blown back by the sheer enormity of the smell. *I thought I'd be used to it by now.* He unslung his round shield from his back, drew his sword, and crept inside. It was a large cavern with many passageways. He held a torch in his shield hand and he made his way up and down the passageways, trying to follow the stench until he found her lair. There was a large pile of gold and gems. *No time for that,* he thought, but there was also something else—the prize he had come for, numerous eggs in various stages. Some were whole, others open, others opening as he watched. There were little black hatchlings lying around. Some old enough to walk a little, and there were several dragon scales left by "Mama."

Koldar thought it was odd that the little creatures were all in different developmental stages. Then he remembered reading something about lizards in one of his mother's books and their various and odd reproductive processes. He combined that thought with the thought that this was a magical creature and pushed the oddity out of his mind. He thought to himself, *Focus on your mission. Well, Blackey you killed my family. Guess it's time to return the favor. He* killed the hatchlings that he saw. They made feeble attempts to spit at him or bite him, but they were from half a foot to two feet in length and couldn't yet fly. He had no problem disposing of them. He picked up several of the unhatched eggs and put them in his pack, then smashed the rest. He also picked up several adult scales before he hurried out of there.

He made his way down the mountainside, slipping and falling a few times, but always keeping the eggs safe. He was almost in a panic now, trying to get down and away as quickly as he could. He pushed hard all that day and into the next, the adrenaline driving him. He made it to the deep of the forest, and he could still hear her wail high above in rage and circling, searching for the intruder. He ran and ran, exhausted beyond all exhaustion. Finally, he tripped, falling into a hole that was partially hidden by branches. There, he gave in and let sleep take him.

He woke up a while later to her screeching. It was dark now. He could hear her swooshing down here and there. He wondered if she had a search pattern or if she was just frantically flying everywhere. He ate a little something and checked to make sure the eggs were still safe before heading out again. He was relying on the darkness and the thick forest trees as a cover, He was grateful she couldn't smell him from where she was.

Weeks later found him still traveling toward The Haven, at some point he had shaken the dragon off his trail. He was so worn out that he now was devoid of any kind of emotion. He only had one thought. *Keep going until I get there.*

Just over four months had passed since Koldar left on his journey to find the dragon's lair. He made it to The Haven, where he was welcomed and fed, and he rested.

CHAPTER 11

Koldar stood in a special chamber of the elven haven. His dagger was set on a beautiful altar made of white marble with silver engravings in magical and elven script. There were several red rubies placed on the alter circling the dagger. He began chanting, holding an egg in one hand and a long silver needle in the other. Galendae, the high elven sorcerer, and the elven mystic looked on in anticipation. The dagger began to glow pale green. Then Koldar stabbed the bottom of the egg with the needle and pulled it out. The contents of the egg began to drain out of the hole as air rushed in the premade hole at the top of the egg. As the contents spilled out, it turned into a black mist which enveloped the dagger. There was the sound of sizzling, and the pale green light changed to a dark, dark red. The steel of the blade turned black, and the leather grip went from green to a dark burgundy color.

Koldar spoke the words, "Koldar of the Black Dragon!" As he spoke the rubies on the alter turned to vapor and went to the dagger. The vapor coalesced into a single point that became a very bright light which began to inscribe on the blade of the dagger. When the light finished inscribing it faded and what was left were the words "Koldar of the Black Dragon" inscribed on the blade in elven script written with the rubies themselves.

Then all was silent. The strain on Koldar was evident, and the elves looked on in amazement.

"You did it!" exclaimed the sorcerer.

* * *

Several days later found Koldar and the elves back in the same room with the altar. The dagger lay at the foot of the altar, along with a spear as black as the dagger's blade. A beautiful sword lay on the altar. It was crafted after the manner of the southern men's long sword, not as the short Northmen blades or the curved blades of the elves. Its blade was also as black as the dagger's. Its dark hilt was expertly created, the ruby accent was a sharp contrast to the darkness of the blade.

The elven sorcerer, the mystic, and several others stood in a circle around Koldar and the altar, chanting in the language of magic. Life essence formed on Koldar's finger, the life essence began to glow bright red. Soon the red glow turned into a red mist that grew and covered Koldar in the vapors. When the drop of essence fell onto the sword, some of the mist followed the drop and entered into the sword. This happened several times, and each time, the mist around Koldar became smaller and smaller until finally, the last drop entered the blade of the sword and the mist around Koldar disappeared completely. Koldar and all those chanting collapsed. The sword not only had the dragon's essence in it, but it also had Koldar's.

* * *

Under Xar's instruction, the men and women of the rescued caravan had been working hard. The first thing they did was rout out the stray animals and pests that had infested the city. They repaired the main gate and started to clean up and repair the rest of the damage. However, Xar had the men focus mainly on battle tactics and weapon skills. He was just beginning to see some improvement and thought this might actually work when he heard a sound that stopped him in his tracks. The lookout at the front gate was blowing the horn of alarm.

He turned to the men he had been instructing and gave orders.

"Archers, to the wall now!" He wished they had some oil to pour over the walls, but the rocks they had gathered would have to do. "It's time to put your training into action!"

Jakahl, one of the men, commented to his friend Calin "So soon?"

"It's time to stop being afraid. Let's do this!" Calin responded, and they both grabbed their quivers and rushed to the main gate.

Xar ran to the top of one of the gate towers to take a look. Black arrows were already starting to fly over the walls. When he got to his perch, he looked out. It was a ragtag army of fell beasts that included goblins, orc archers, some mountain trolls, and other little creatures.

They must have been waiting for this city to be inhabited again just so they could loot it and tear it down. They are probably starving in a mountain cavern nearby and thought we looked like dinner. Taking note of the fact that they were outnumbered, he gave more orders to the men he had been training. They were a little hesitant. *Definitely not the great Northmen warriors I'm used to.*

"All right, men! It's time to defend your right to survive! These beasts are hungry and think we will be easy prey. Let's show them we are not their food!"

Calin responded with a yell and continued running to his position near Spit on the wall. The rest of the men followed suit, finally determined to fight for their home.

* * *

The battle was going poorly. The orc archers rained arrows down upon the city, making it hard for the defenders to get off accurate shots. This also paved the way for the mountain trolls to start ramming the front gate. There were four of them that would take turns ramming with a large tree. Some archers were able to hit them, but their hide was tough enough that it was not yet a deterrent, and the rocks being thrown down from the crenels were just as ineffective against the massive bodies.

The hastily repaired gate was beginning to buckle under the onslaught. Xar was losing hope, but he shouted encouragement. He had his large axe and was just starting to run down to meet the trolls when he felt the wind pick up significantly. Then he heard a horn blast. Looking out over the parapets, he saw a very welcome sight.

Behind the army of fell beasts stood Koldar, Galendae, the elf Alanthulus, a rogue barbarian friend of Koldar's named Karazhon Zhacor and his group of men, and Cahlista the huntress. A small group, but all very skilled in battle.

Koldar's tunic was black with a red trim that simulated the crenels of a battlement. Over his tunic was armor that looked to be made of black dragon scales. He wore a black cape that had a red trim around the edges of the mantle. The slight almost unnoticeable breeze that had been naturally occurring now changed direction and started to grow in strength. As the wind continued to pick up, it blew off Koldar's hood, revealing his black helmet. His hands were in the air, and he was chanting. Galendae blew the horn again. The wind was blowing straight north and continued growing in strength blowing right into the faces of the beasts. Now shooting into the wind, the orcish arrows were missing their marks or unable to breach the parapets at all. This gave the archers on the wall a reprieve, and they were able to get off more shots. The wind going in the direction they were shooting actually carried the arrows a little farther than they normally would have gone, and more and more beasts were falling dead, pierced by the defending arrows.

The beasts, now a little confused, began to break slightly. Koldar unslung his new shield which he had made and hefted it. It was a teardrop shield, a hybrid of the Northman round shield and the Southern kite shield. It was made of black dragon scales, and he had covered it with a cloth bearing his standard. Near him, Galendae blew the horn again, and then planted Koldar's banner in the ground where he stood. It was flat across the top and came down in two points, a black background with a disembodied dragon neck and head and two disembodied dragon wings. They were grayish silver in color, with a red trim.

Then Koldar drew his sword, black as black could be with a deep red glow about the blade and a swirling red mist emanating from it. Galendae drew his sword, which glowed green. Alanthulus lowered his eight-foot pike. Karazhon Zhacor readied his sword and shield, as did his men and Cahlista shouldered her bow and instead drew two swords. Koldar yelled and they all charged into battle, handing out death among the fell beasts. The arrows of the defenders continued to fall. The orcs, now finding their arrows ineffective, drew their swords and turned to try to stop Koldar's advance.

The trolls now were frantically trying to break down the gate. Two of the trolls held up trees to cover themselves and their two companions who were still working on battering down the barrier. This protected them somewhat from the large volley of arrows that were now a threat to their operation.

Xar knew that they would soon be successful if not stopped. He threw down his axe from the battlement about fifty feet east of the gate, then jumped down the twenty-foot height himself. He landed in a soft grassy spot he had picked out, rolled and popped up seamlessly. He grabbed his massive axe and charged. He came upon one of the trolls that was covering himself and his companion with a tree. In one motion, he swung at the troll's leg, crippling him, then brought the axe down into his back. The thickness of the hide was fairly protective, but against Xar's strength and mighty axe, the troll went down wounded.

The two trolls using the tree as a battering ram now dropped their burden and turned their attention to Xar. The fourth troll continued to use his tree to block the arrows as best he could.

Xar fought the beasts, their massive clubs pounding him while he slashed back with his axe cutting deep into them. The fourth troll now started attacking Xar as well, doing his best to ignore the arrows coming down. It seemed now that the trolls were gaining the advantage. Suddenly, Xar heard a hissing sound and smelled something awful. Looking around, he saw a black smoldering spear which had just pierced through one of the trolls. As the troll fell, Xar looked to see Koldar standing a little way off, obviously the one who threw the spear. Koldar was soon enveloped by orcs and Xar had to continue fighting the trolls on his own.

Soon, the beasts decided that the meal was not worth this effort and began to retreat into the forest and mountains, one of the trolls leading the way. Xar tried to follow, but the first troll he had crippled tripped him by swinging a club at his feet. Not being able to pursue the other trolls, he got back up and finished that creature off. Koldar let the others go, feeling they had made their point.

Xar and Koldar embraced, and a cheer went up from the caravan refugees.

Epilogue 1

A priest of Cyros, dressed in bright yellow robes with red trim, stood facing east with his ten-year-old son. "Now follow my movements so that when the time is right, you will be ready." The boy nodded in solemn reverence and understanding. Then the priest stretched his arms down with his empty palms facing forward and said, "Ignite!"

In an instant, he was holding a sword in his right hand, and on his left arm was an elongated oval shield, both made of nothing but pure flame. Then methodically and gracefully, the priest began to move his arms and legs in a slow, dance-like motion, his son shadowing him almost perfectly.

After a time, the priest said, "Dowse!" and his flaming shield and sword vanished. He lifted back his cowl and let it fall gently on his back, and he turned to his son. "All right now, Arius," he encouraged. "It is time to pray. Go ahead and say what is in your heart."

The priest, still standing, bowed his head. The boy knelt and prayed aloud, "Dear Cyros, I thank thee for the blessings of light and truth which thou hast provided. I pray thee, dear Cyros, to help me to be able to find a lost soul that I can help find his way through this life, that he and I together might find eternal joy and rest in Ahl's presence . . ."

Epilogue 2

A baron, at least in his own mind, walked down the hall of his little castle, holding his hands to his ears in an attempt to block out the crying of a little boy. He burst into his wife's chambers and yelled, "Can't you get that child to be quiet!?"

"I am trying, Your Grace," she responded.

"It's difficult to plan my next attack with all his racket filling the halls. I need to go capture some more slaves!"

"He is terribly frightened, Your Grace, and keeps yelling for his da. The only thing I have learned is that his name is Ahrik."

The End
(of the Beginning)

Appendix of the Powers

AHL
THE FATHER
The High God and Father of the gods and
the spirits of the races

Cyros- God of light and truth
He is the first born of Ahl and is the head god of Ahl's god children. He has oracles on the world.

Arizon- Goddess of freedom and justice.
She is Cyros' twin and former lover to Kalaar.

Sleros- God of the sea.
He is Cyros' brother and the sea reflects his fickle nature.

Ahslyanus- God of life and fertility and merry making.
He is Cyros' brother and father of the elves (their bodies, not their spirits). He is married to L'thandril.

Karr- God of earth working
He is Cyros' brother and the father of the dwarves (their bodies, not their spirits).

Kalaar- God of death and decay (originally that decay which brings new life).
He is Cyros' brother and the father of the strife of the gods and the evils of the world.
He has fallen from his place and is now simply the god of death and decay, nothing new coming from it.
He is also known as **Death**.

Andilynn- Goddess of nature (plants and animals) and patroness of the fairy world.
She is Cyros' sister (Skeris' twin) and Kelthros' lover.

Skeris- God of the sky and fowls.
He is Andilynn's twin.

This is the family of Ahl. He and his spouse raised these from infancy before entering the ways of forever.

The following gods are friends, lovers or children of the *Ahlspring*.

Kelthros- God of sport and the hunt.
He is Andilynn's lover and thinks fighting is a game, even when locked in mortal combat.

Pyron-God of fire, hate, rebellion, and fear.
He is Cyros' first child and was one of Kalaar's two head generals during the God Wars.

Relue- God of law and order, the protector of oaths.
He is Cyros' son. He was imprisoned in Kalaar's sword during the God Wars.

Dradok- God of blood and war.
He is Kalaar's first child and was Kalaar's other chief general during the God Wars.

Viktroath- God of the Struggle and Victory.
He is Kelthros' illegitimate son and was Slarius' tutor.

Steth- God of thieves and assassins.
He is Kalaar's son.

Xerxon- God of Chaos.
He was a tagalong friend of Kelthros'. He was the first to discover the spirit of chaos in the void.

Masaelisa- Goddess of torture, pain, and suffering.

Kelara- Goddess of wit and luck.

Surisis- Goddess of magic and mystery.
She is called the mother of the Mystics.

L'thandril- Goddess of music and poetry, the arts and the stars.
She is Ahslyanus' spouse and the mother of the elves (their bodies).

Swernjudd- God of wisdom, intelligence, literature, and learning
He also has oracles on the world.

Leandil- Goddess of beauty and love.
She is Andilynn's daughter.

Sortfynas- God of greed, appetite, and lust.

Rethex- God of tyranny, suppression, and control. (Lord of the Tyrants).

Krom- God of duty, loyalty, and obedience.

Pethres- God of success, plenty, trade, wealth, and money.

Agora- Goddess of peace, virtue, goodness, kindness and brotherly love.
She is Cyros' wife.

Kalaina- Goddess of vice, darkness, spite, and ill intentions.

Lydain- Goddess of healing.

Azendus- God of science, medicine and alchemy.

Shade- Goddess of deception and illusion, trickery and imagination.

Serrel- God of endurance and trials and the unfortunate.

Arman- God of rulership and power (The Lord of the Kings).

Aralynn- Goddess of cold (The Snow Queen).
2 main Hahlier: one more evil in nature and one more good in nature. (they are both minor deity status)

Hahlier are minor powers. Each Hahlier serves a major power.

www.thelosttalesofaralon.com

CREDITS
And a very special thanks to these very talented people! All three of whom were wonderful to work with! I highly recommend all of them!

Draco Herrera
Front cover illustrator and in-book character illustrator
cherreradraw@gmail.com

Rowan North
Rowan North Illustrations
In-book Illustrations pages: 18, 38, 47, 51
RowanNorthIllustrations@gmail.com
https://www.facebook.com/Rowansart/
http://rowannorth.deviantart.com/

Jonathan R Briggs
Graphic Design and Artworking
jonathanbriggs1980@gmail.com

Also a very special thanks to all those who supported me and worked on this behind the scenes!

97751276R00033

Made in the USA
Columbia, SC
14 June 2018